WORLD CHAMP

THIS
WORLD OF NORM
BOOK BELONGS TO:

muppet!

VALUE
LAND
Toilet
Paper

hmmmm...

Absolute

mayhem begin!

ORCHARD BOOKS

First published in Great Britain in 2016 by The Watts Publishing Group

1 3 5 7 9 10 8 6 4 2

Text © Jonathan Meres 2016
Illustrations © Donough O'Malley 2016

The moral rights of the author and illustrator have been asserted.

A CIP catalogue record for this book
is available from the British Library.

UK ISBN: 978 1 40834 287 9
Export ISBN: 978 1 40834 371 5

Printed and bound in Great Britain by
CPI Group (UK) Ltd, Croydon, CR0 4YY

The paper and board used in this book are
made from wood from responsible sources.

MIX
Paper from
responsible sources
FSC® C104740
www.fsc.org

Orchard Books
An imprint of
Hachette Children's Group
Part of The Watts Publishing Group Limited
Carmelite House
50 Victoria Embankment
London EC4Y 0DZ

An Hachette UK Company
www.hachette.co.uk

www.hachettechildrens.co.uk

JONATHAN MERES

WELCOME TO THE WORLD OF NORM

ORCHARD

To World Book Day.
Thanks for having me
x

CHAPTER 1

Norm knew it was going to be one of those days when he woke up to find a half-Polish Cockapoo sat on his head. Which admittedly was better than finding *half* a Polish Cockapoo sat on his head. But not all that much. And not that Norm actually *realised* he had a half-Polish Cockapoo sat on his head. He just thought that for some reason it was unusually dark in his bedroom. As well as unbe-flipping-*lievably* smelly.

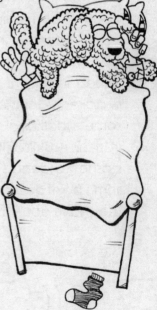

"Phwoar!" said Norm, wafting his hand in front of his face. Or, at least, wafting his hand in front of the place where his face usually was.

Woof, went John sleepily.

"Uh? What?" said Norm, suddenly becoming aware of his predicament and the fact that if he didn't do something about it pretty flipping quickly, there was every chance that he'd be overcome by fumes. And, boy, were there plenty of fumes! In fact, if Norm wasn't very much mistaken, John had recently released some additional fumes, mere millimetres from his nostrils. Either that, or someone had stashed a dead squirrel under his pillow at some point during the night. And why would they have done that? wondered Norm. But

6

that wasn't the point. The point was that he needed to act fast if he didn't want his day to go from bad to catas-flipping-trophic.

"GERROFFME!!!" bellowed Norm like a buffalo with bellyache, somehow finding the strength to raise himself up and at the same time tip John onto the floor, where he promptly curled up and fell fast asleep again, as if he didn't have a single care in the world. Unlike Norm, who had more than his fair share of cares.

Norm glared venomously at the dozing dog. *He* would have *loved* to have fallen fast asleep again, but he was wide awake now. It was so flipping unfair. But then, what wasn't? In Norm's world pretty much *everything* was unfair – and had been for as long as he could remember. Well, certainly since his stupid little brothers had been born anyway. Up until then everything had been fine. Whatever he'd wanted, he'd got. Which, as far as Norm

was concerned, was precisely how things were **meant** to be. The world had revolved around **him** and him alone. He'd been the centre of his mum and dad's universe. He only had to cough and they'd be running around like headless chickens, frantically scouring medical books and Googling for potential deadly diseases he may have picked up at nursery. Not that headless chickens could actually read, of course. Or Google, for that matter. But that wasn't the point either, thought Norm. The point was that things had gone rapidly downhill ever since Brian and Dave had been around. And, ever since his dad had lost his job and they'd had to move to this stupid little house and started eating own-brand flipping Coco Pops instead of **proper** Coco Pops, things hadn't so much gone rapidly downhill as plummeted headfirst over a flipping cliff.

"Oh, **there** you are!" said Brian, suddenly bursting through the door.

Norm regarded his middle brother with a look of barely concealed contempt. "Where did you **think** I was?"

"What?" said Brian. "No, not **you**, Norman. John!"

"Uh? Oh, right," said Norm, as Brian picked the dog up.

"Yes, I was looking for you, wasn't I, Johnny-wonny?" said Brian in a funny baby voice. "Yes, I wassy-wassy."

John, now fully awake again, responded by

licking Brian full in the face.

"Aw, that is ***disgusting***!" said Norm.

"No, it's not," said Brian. "He's perfectly clean!"

"What?" said Norm. "No, I meant it's disgusting for the dog, not you."

"Ha ha, very funny," said Brian, putting John back down on the floor.

"And how about flipping knocking first, by the way?"

"Knocking?" said Brian.

"On the door?" said Norm. "Before you come in?"

"Why should I knock?"

Norm looked at Brian as if he was something

he'd just scraped off the bottom of his shoe. "What do you **mean**, why should you knock? Because it's my flipping room, that's why!"

"Erm, well, not **really**," said Brian.

"What do you **mean**, not really?" said Norm, getting more and more exasperated.

"Well, I mean it's Mum and Dad's house really, isn't it?" said Brian. "So, technically, it's **their** room, not yours."

"Yeah," said Norm. "And technically you've got three seconds to get out of it."

"Or else what?" said Brian.

"Or else..." began Norm.

"What?" said Brian.

It was a good question actually, thought Norm. Or else what? Or else he said something so witheringly mean and sarcastic that Brian simply exploded into tears and was never ever quite the same again? Because Norm knew he couldn't lay so much as finger on him without Brian running off and blabbing to his mum and dad. And **then** what would happen? Norm would be punished in one way or another. And what was the likeliest form of punishment? Being grounded, that was what. And that would be an abso-flipping-lute **disaster**. Because as Norm had just remembered, today was Saturday. And Saturdays meant one thing and one thing alone: biking with Mikey!

"Well?" said Brian. "Else what?"

Norm sighed. "Nothing."

"Didn't think so," said Brian, disappearing out onto the landing. "Come on."

Norm looked around but John was nowhere to be seen and had presumably gone already.

"Not John. You," said Brian, sticking his head back round the door.

"Uh?" said Norm.

"I meant to say," said Brian. "Dad wants to see you. Downstairs. Now."

"What about?" said Norm.

"Don't know," said Brian, disappearing again.

Gordon flipping **Bennet**, thought Norm, getting up and trudging slowly after his brother, with all the enthusiasm of a slug with an attitude problem.

CHAPTER 2

"Dad?" called Norm from the foot of the stairs.

"In here!" yelled Norm's dad from the direction of the kitchen.

Norm breathed a huge sigh of relief. Whatever it was that his dad wanted to see him about, couldn't be all *that* bad. Because whenever he was in *really* big trouble, or there was some kind of *major* problem, Norm was usually summonsed to the front room, to find his parents waiting to pass judgement like a king and queen from medieval times.

Of course, that didn't necessarily mean that everything was going to be fine either,

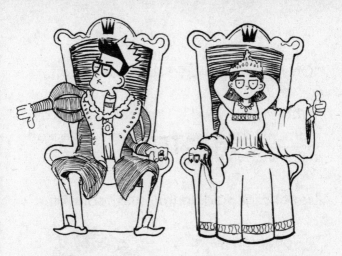

and that Norm was going to live happily
ever after, like in some stupid book. He
knew better than to expect **that**. He hadn't
been born **yesterday**, as Grandpa would
say. And frankly it would be weird if he **had**
been born yesterday. But that wasn't the
point. The point was that Norm was nearly
thirteen. He knew the score. And he nearly
always lost.

"Norman?" yelled Norm's dad.

"Yeah?"

"Are you coming, or what?"

"Oh, right. Yeah," said Norm, setting off.

"What kept you?" said Norm's dad a moment later, when Norm appeared in the kitchen doorway.

"Er, nothing," said Norm. "I was just thinking."

"I wondered what that burning smell was," grinned Dave, between mouthfuls of own-brand cereal.

"Shut up, Dave, you little freak," hissed Norm.

"Language!" said Dave.

"Now, now, you two," said Norm's mum from the sink. "Why can't you just get on?"

"How long have you got?" muttered Norm.

"I thought that was the toast," said Brian, sitting next to Dave at the table.

"Thought **what** was the toast?" said Dave.

"That burning smell."

"That was a joke, Brian."

"Oh, right," said Brian.

"Dare I ask **what** you were thinking?" said Norm's dad, between sips of own-brand instant coffee.

Norm shrugged. "Dunno. Can if you want."

Norm's dad looked at Norm expectantly. "Well?"

"What?" said Norm.

"What were you thinking?"

"Oh, right," said Norm. "Nothing much."

"Nothing much?"

Norm shook his head.

"Excellent," said Norm's dad. "Glad we got *that* cleared up."

Brian pulled a face. "Got *what* cleared up?"

"I think Dad's being sarcastic," whispered Dave out the corner of his mouth.

"Oh, I see," said Brian.

"I expect you're wondering what I wanted to see you about?" said Norm's dad.

"Er, yeah," said Norm. "I expect I am."

"Which do you want first? The good news or the bad news?"

Norm sighed. So there **was** bad news then. He flipping knew it.

"Well?" said Norm's dad.

Norm thought for a moment. What difference did it make, if he got the bad news immediately, or if he delayed it a bit? It was like trying to delay the flipping weather. It was still going to happen sooner or later.

"Come on," said Norm's dad impatiently. "We haven't got all day, you know."

Brian looked puzzled. "But it's Saturday."

"So?" said Dave.

"So, technically, we **have** got all day."

"Come on, love," said Norm's mum, looking directly at Norm.

"What?"

"Hurry up and **choose**!"

Norm suddenly felt frozen with indecision, like a rabbit caught in car headlights. He might as well toss a mental coin. Heads for good. Tails for bad.

"**Now**?" said Norm's dad.

"Tails," said Norm.

Norm's dad pulled a face. "Pardon?"

"Erm, I mean I'll have the good news first please, Dad."

"We're going to IKEA."

"WHAAAAAAAAAAT?" squawked Norm.

"I knew you'd be pleased," said Norm's dad.

Pleased? thought Norm. What planet was his dad actually **on**? Clearly not the same one that **he** was on. Going to IKEA was at the very top of his list of all-time worst flipping **nightmares**. Not that Norm actually **had** a list of all-time worst nightmares. But if he did, it would be right up there. Even higher than the recurring one where he was chased down the street by a bunch of flesh-eating zombie badgers. Not to mention the one where he was standing onstage giving a speech to the whole school, before suddenly realising that he was totally naked. And **definitely** not to mention the one where there was a worldwide shortage of pizza toppings.

"Which brings me to the **bad** news," said Norm's dad.

Bad news? thought Norm. What could **possibly** be worse than being dragged around a never-ending sea of shelving

units, sofas and flipping wardrobes all day?
Staying **overnight** in IKEA and being forced
to do exactly the same thing the next day?
And the next day? And the day after **that**?
And the day after that? Until all your days
started blurring into one and you ended
up going stark-raving mad? No way out.
Trapped for ever in some kind of futuristic,
post-apoca-whatsit world, like one of those
Xbox games, or a flipping science-fiction
movie or something? Norm could see the
poster now: "In IKEA, no one can hear you
scream!"

"You can't come with us."

Norm stared at his dad for a second as
if he'd just started talking in some kind of
strange alien language. Had he just said
what he **thought** he'd just said?

"Pardon, Dad?"

"I said you can't come, Norman. To IKEA."

Norm continued to stare. So his dad really **had** just said what he thought he'd said. He just wasn't sure how to react. Because his dad had also just said that this was the **bad** news. And this wasn't **bad** at all. This was the complete polar **opposite** of bad news. This was very **good** news indeed.

"I hope you're not **too** disappointed?" said Norm's dad, concern etched across his forehead.

"I'll get over it," said Norm.

"Sure?" said Norm's dad.

Norm nodded and smiled bravely. Or, at least, **tried** to smile bravely. Which wasn't easy, because what he **really** wanted to do was whoop and holler and run down the street high-fiving random passers-by and inviting them all back for a massive party. Not that he actually **would**, of course. Because for a start they didn't have any

decent food in the house. And anyway, the first thing Norm was going to do when the others eventually left for IKEA – without him – was jump on his bike and head over to Mikey's!

"Sorry, love," said Norm's mum. "But **someone's** got to wait in."

"Uh?" said Norm, screwing his face up until it looked like a wrinkled balloon. "Wait **in**?"

"For the parcel."

"What parcel?" said Norm, getting more and more confused.

"Oh, just something I've ordered from one of the shopping channels."

Of course, thought Norm. He might have flipping known. And knowing **his** mum, that could mean just about **anything**. From striped paint, to some stupid gadget for straightening bananas or something, there was nothing – literally **nothing** – she wouldn't order off one of the flipping shopping channels. But that wasn't the point, thought Norm. The point was that never mind **banana**-shaped, his day was about to go seriously **pear**-shaped if he didn't do something about it. But what **could** he do about it? That was the question.

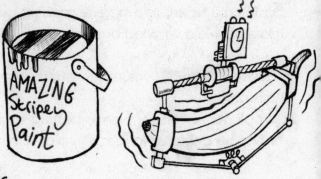

"What time's it going to get here?" said Norm.

"That's the thing," said Norm's mum.

"What's the thing?" said Norm.

"We don't know. It could be anytime."

"But..." began Norm.

"What?" said Norm's mum.

"I'm supposed to be going biking with Mikey!"

"Well, I'm afraid you can't," said Norm's dad. "You're staying here and that's all there is to it."

"Flipping *brilliant*," muttered Norm under his breath.

"What was that, Norman?" said Norm's

dad, the vein on the side of his head beginning to throb – a sure-fire sign that he was starting to get stressed. Not that Norm noticed. Not that Norm **ever** noticed.

"Nothing," said Norm.

Brian pulled a face. "Why's that brilliant?"

"Shut up, Brian!" spat Norm.

"Charming," said Brian.

"Look, I know it's frustrating, love," said Norm's mum. "But we couldn't very well leave your brothers, could we? They're much too young."

"Yeah, Norman!" said Dave.

"Yeah, Norman!" echoed Brian.

Norm looked at his two little brothers. He wished *he* could leave them. Permanently.

"Tenner," said Norm.

"Pardon?" said Norm's mum.

"I'll do it for a tenner."

"You'll do *what* for a tenner?" said Norm's dad.

"Stay at home," said Norm.

Everything suddenly went very quiet. As if someone had just hoovered up all the sounds.

"I'll pretend I didn't hear that, Norman," said Norm's dad calmly, getting up and leaving.

Norm watched him go. His dad could pretend all he wanted. But he'd still said it.

"Don't worry, love," said Norm's mum. "We'll make it up to you somehow."

"Really?" said Norm, brightening just a teensy bit. "How?"

"We'll think of something," said Norm's mum, heading for the door. "Now come on, you two. We don't want to keep Dad waiting, do we?"

"'kay, Mum!" sang Brian and Dave in unison, jumping up and following.

Norm sighed. Under the circumstances, it was just about all he could flipping do.

CHAPTER 3

Just because Norm had to stay **at** home, didn't mean he actually had to stay **in** home. Which was why, less than two minutes after his parents, his brothers and John the half-Polish Cockapoo had piled into their sorry excuse for a car and driven off down the street, Norm was getting his bike out of the garage.

What was that expression? wondered Norm. Every clown has a silver lining? Something like that. Grandpa would know. Grandpa knew **loads** of expressions from the olden days. But whatever. Didn't really matter. Norm **kind** of knew what it meant. It meant that even in a **bad** situation, something **good** might still come out of it. Which was usually a load of old nonsense as far as **Norm** was concerned. Because in Norm's experience, some situations were just flipping rubbish. In fact, in **Norm's** experience, **most** situations were flipping rubbish. But in this **particular** instance, it was actually true. OK, so he was having to stay at home and not go biking with Mikey, which was what he **really** wished he was doing. But he could still do a few tricks. At least he'd be **on** his bike. That was all that mattered. Because biking was just about the most important thing in Norm's life. In fact, never mind just **about** – biking **was** the most important thing in Norm's life. End of. Full stop. No terms. No conditions. It just flipping **was**. And it would **continue** to be, at least until Norm achieved his dream of one day becoming World Mountain Biking

Champion, however long *that* might take.

Somewhere in the distance, a clock struck ten. Norm had no idea how long the others would be away for. But he knew that he should really make the most of the peace and quiet and do some serious practising. Starting right now with a trackstand.

"Hello, **Norman**!" said an all too familiar voice from the other side of the fence, the split second Norm got on his bike and began balancing.

Gordon flipping **Bennet**, thought Norm, wobbling about and immediately having to put his feet back on the ground again. So much for peace and flipping quiet, then. Just because Chelsea was the world's most annoying next door neighbour didn't mean she had to pop up like a flipping jack in a box every time he so much as stuck his big toe outside, did it? It was **so** annoying. Although, admittedly not **quite** so annoying as the way Chelsea insisted on always overemphasising his name like it was the most hilarious thing she'd ever flipping heard.

"Not talking, then?" said Chelsea.

"Do I have a choice?" grumbled Norm.

"Now, now, **Norman**. That's not very nice."

Norm sighed. Perhaps if he was vaguely pleasant, she'd go away again? But being even **vaguely** pleasant to Chelsea was easier said than done. She was, without a doubt, one of the most obnoxious people he knew. And that **included** Brian.

"What are you **doing**?" Chelsea asked, as Norm took his feet off the ground again and started balancing. Or at least **tried** to.

"Trackstand," said Norm.

"Pardon?" said Chelsea.

"It's called a trackstand."

"What is?"

"What I'm doing."

"Why?"

"Dunno," said Norm. "It just is."

"No," said Chelsea. "I mean, **_why_** are you doing it?"

"Just am," said Norm, just about managing to bite his tongue and resist his natural urge to tell her to mind her own flipping business.

"Looks a bit pointless, to me," said Chelsea.

"Yeah, well, it's not," said Norm.

"If you say so, **Norman**."

Norm was not only finding it more and more difficult to keep his balance, he was finding it more and more difficult not to get **seriously** wound up. Just what **was** it about Chelsea that he found so deeply and intensely irritating? Apart from every single thing that she said? And every single thing that she did? And the way she popped up every time he set foot on the flipping drive? And the way she pronounced his name? But apart from that... Norm couldn't quite put his finger on it.

"Are you ever going to go anywhere?"

"What?" said Norm, wobbling uncontrollably and putting his feet on the ground again.

"I was just wondering whether you're actually going to **go** anywhere," said Chelsea. "Or whether you're just going to stay there, doing bandstands, or hat stands, or whatever they're called?"

"**Track**stands," said Norm through gritted teeth. "And, anyway, I **can't** go anywhere."

Chelsea looked puzzled. "What do you mean, you can't go anywhere? Are you **stuck**?"

Norm sighed. "No, I'm not **stuck**. I mean I've got to stay here."

"Oh, I see," said Chelsea. "Why?"

"Because everyone else has gone to IKEA."

"So?"

"So I've got to wait for some stupid parcel to be delivered."

"Right," said Chelsea.

"*That's* why I can't go anywhere," said Norm.

"Hmmm," said Chelsea. "And would you *like* to go somewhere?"

"Seriously?"

"Seriously."

"Yeah," said Norm.

"Where?" said Chelsea.

"Biking with Mikey!" said Norm, like this was the most stupid question ever in the entire history of stupid questions.

"All right, *Norman*!" said Chelsea. "Keep your hair on. How was I supposed to know *that*? I'm not *psychic*!"

Obviously not, thought Norm. Because if Chelsea **was** psychic, she'd have known not to bother talking to him in the first flipping place.

Neither said anything for a while. It was as if someone had put their conversation on pause.

"What?" said Norm, eventually.

"Nothing," said Chelsea. "I'm just thinking, that's all."

"What about?"

"You really want to know?"

"Yeah," said Norm.

"I'm thinking that I'm not actually doing anything today."

Gordon flipping **Bennet**, thought Norm, beginning to feel panic rising up inside him like water in a blocked drain. Was Chelsea really about to suggest that they hung out together today? That they actually spent *time* with one another? Or worse? Because if so, he'd better start thinking up some excuses pretty flipping quickly.

"So I could keep a lookout for the parcel being delivered."

"Sorry, what?" said Norm.

"You heard."

Chelsea was right. Norm **had** heard. He just wasn't sure that he actually **believed** what he heard.

"You mean..."

"You could go biking!" said Chelsea. "Exactly!"

Norm pulled a face. "But..."

"What?" said Chelsea.

"It's just that..."

"What?"

"I dunno," said Norm.

"Look, you don't **have** to, if you don't **want** to," said Chelsea. "It's just an idea. I'm not going to **make** you! No one's going to **make** you!"

"But..."

"**What**?"

"Why?" said Norm.

"**Why**?" said Chelsea.

Norm nodded.

Chelsea thought for a moment. "I'm not sure. Perhaps I like you."

"**What**?" said Norm as if Chelsea had just casually mentioned that she'd been a llama in a previous life.

"Not in *that* kind of way," said Chelsea. "*Obviously*."

Norm was confused. As far as he was aware, there was only one way that a girl *could* like a boy. And it was *exactly* that kind of way. The thought of which was even *more* gross than waking up to find a farting dog on your head. And another thing. Why did she have to say 'obviously'?

"I don't get it."

Chelsea grinned. "There's nothing to get, *Norman*!" she said. "Just *do* it before I change my mind!"

Never mind *her* mind, thought Norm. *His* mind was humming like a flipping microwave. Why would *Chelsea*, of all people, want to do *him* a favour? If it was the other way round, would *he* do the same for *her*? Not flipping likely. He'd sooner snog a snake than do any kind of

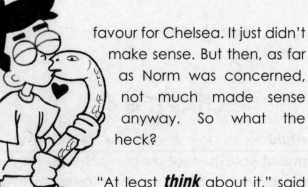

favour for Chelsea. It just didn't make sense. But then, as far as Norm was concerned, not much made sense anyway. So what the heck?

"At least **think** about it," said Chelsea.

"Already have," said Norm.

"And?"

"Thanks very much!" said Norm, pedalling down the drive and heading off along the street.

"YOU'RE WELCOME, **NORMAN**!" yelled Chelsea.

But it was too late. Norm had already gone.

CHAPTER 4

Free at last! thought Norm, as if he'd just
broken out of a
top-security prison
and not simply left
his own house and
cycled down the
road, towards Mikey's.
But to Norm it almost
felt as if he **had** just
broken out of
prison. The relief
was immense.
Like some kind of
massive weight had
been lifted off his
shoulders. Or he'd
just woken up to
find that he really

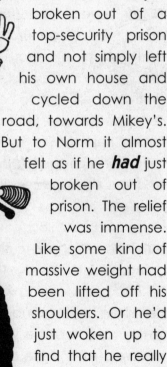

was an only child after all, and that all the years since Brian and Dave were born had just been a bad dream.

But Norm didn't **only** feel relief. Because he still didn't **fully** understand why Chelsea had done what she'd done. She can't **really** have offered to look out for the parcel, just to be **nice**, could she? What kind of freak of nature would actually do **that**? Surely there had to be **some** kind of motive? There had to be **something** in it for her, didn't there? Because if there **wasn't**, then Chelsea was even **more** annoying than Norm already **thought** she was. And **that** was flipping saying something.

Norm was so lost in thought that he temporarily forgot to look where he was going. Which was a pity really, because if he **had** been looking where he was going, he might have actually **seen** the pothole in the road that he was heading straight towards. And if he'd actually **seen** the pothole, he might well have decided to try and jump **across** it, rather than ride straight **over** it.

"OOOF!!!" went Norm as his bike came to an abrupt and juddering halt. Unfortunately – or possibly **fortunately** – Norm himself **didn't** come to an abrupt halt and promptly parted company with his bike, before flying through the air and landing in a crumpled heap a little further on down the road.

"Gordon flipping **Bennet**!" said Norm, getting up and dusting himself down, apparently none the worse for wear.

"Typical," said a voice. "Never got a camera with you when you really **need** one."

"Uh?" said Norm, turning around to see Grandpa holding a watering can and looking at him through the allotments fence. "Oh. Hi, Grandpa. Didn't see you there."

"No, you didn't, did you?" said Grandpa. "And you didn't see that hole, either."

Obviously, thought Norm. Did Grandpa think he'd crashed **deliberately**? He'd had no idea he was even anywhere near the allotments, let alone that he'd been heading for a gap in the road the size of the flipping Grand Canyon!

"You all right?"

"Yeah, I think so," said Norm, flexing his fingers and bending over to touch his toes.

"Pity," said Grandpa.

Norm pulled a face. "What?"

"Pity I didn't film it. We could've sent it to one of those funny clip shows on TV."

"Oh, right, I see what you mean," said Norm.

"Could've made a bit of money," said Grandpa. "Enough to pay for a whole new **bike**, never mind a new **wheel**."

"Sorry, what?" said Norm.

"Well, look at it," said Grandpa, with a tilt of his head.

Norm swivelled around and immediately saw what Grandpa was referring to. The front wheel of his bike was so badly buckled and twisted, it looked more like a miniature roller coaster at a teensy little funfair for mice.

"NOOOOOO!!!" wailed Norm like a character from a horror movie. But unfortunately, as far as **Norm** was concerned, this was no movie. This was really happening. Or, strictly speaking, already **had** happened.

"You can't ride that," said Grandpa.

"No, *really*?" said Norm.

"Are you being sarcastic, Norman?" said Grandpa. "Because if you are. . ."

Grandpa stopped mid-sentence.

"What, Grandpa?" said Norm.

"Pardon?"

"If I'm being sarcastic, you'll *what*?"

Grandpa thought for a moment. "I can't think of anything. I'll phone you later."

Norm couldn't help grinning. Even though he was in no mood to. But Grandpa was really funny. And, right now, Norm didn't have all that much to laugh about. In fact, right now, Norm didn't have *anything* to laugh about. Quite the opposite. He'd just pranged his bike so badly that unless something bordering on the miraculous happened, he wasn't going to be able to go riding with Mikey after all. Well, *he* hadn't pranged his bike. But the flipping *road* had. Either way, thought Norm, it looked very much as if biking was off the menu for the rest of the day. And either way, thought Norm, it was *so* flipping unfair.

"Well?" said Grandpa.

"What?" said Norm.

"What are you waiting for?"

It was a good question actually, thought Norm. What *was* he waiting for? For a genie to magically appear out of Grandpa's watering can and make everything right again? Because if so, he had a feeling he was in for a flipping long wait.

52

"Earth to Norman. Come in, please, Norman," said Grandpa, covering his nose and mouth with his free hand and putting on an American accent.

"Uh?" said Norm.

"Do you want me to try and fix it, or not?" said Grandpa.

"My *bike*?" said Norm.

"No," said Grandpa. "Your fashion sense."

Norm looked blankly at Grandpa for several seconds before, eventually, Grandpa's eyes began to crinkle ever so slightly in the corners. Which was the closest Grandpa ever came to smiling.

"Of *course* I mean your bike, you numpty."

"Whoa!" said Norm, the penny finally dropping. "Thanks, Grandpa!"

"I can't do it through the fence, though."

"What?"

"You'll need to bring it in here," said Grandpa, turning around and heading for his shed.

"Oh, right," said Norm, picking his bike up and wheeling it towards the entrance of the allotments. Or *trying* to wheel it, anyway. Which wasn't easy, what with the wheel being wonky.

"Numpty," muttered Grandpa, before finally disappearing through the door.

Norm grinned as he watched him go. Who needed *stupid* genies, when you had a magic grandpa?

CHAPTER 5

"Right then," said Grandpa, bending down and peering at Norm's front wheel. Or rather, the front wheel on Norm's *bike*. "What have we got here?"

Norm looked. Or at least *tried* to look. But it was pretty gloomy in Grandpa's shed, despite it being bright and sunny outside. Not that that seemed to bother Grandpa. But then Grandpa was *used* to being in the shed. And Norm wasn't.

"Know what I think, Norman?"

"What, Grandpa?" said Norm.

"I think it's definitely buckled."

Brilliant, thought Norm. He could have told Grandpa *that* himself! What other earth-shattering revelations was he about to discover? That night followed day? That money didn't *really* grow on trees? That people in glasshouses shouldn't throw stones, or whatever that expression was? Though why anyone would actually want to live in a glass house in the first place, let alone throw stones in one, was a mystery to Norm. Quite apart from all the health and safety implications. But that wasn't the point, thought Norm. The point was that he already *knew* the flipping wheel was buckled! A short-sighted *bat* could see that the flipping wheel was buckled! This wasn't exactly breaking news.

NEWS FLASH

"There's only one thing for it," said Grandpa.

There is? thought Norm. And what was that? he wondered.

"Give it a good whack," said Grandpa.

Norm stared at Grandpa as if Grandpa had just casually announced he was giving up his allotment and joining a death-thrash metal band instead. He surely wasn't **serious**, was he?

"Sorry, Grandpa. Did you say..."

"Whack it," said Grandpa, nodding. "Yes, I did."

Norm looked horrified. "But..."

"What?" said Grandpa.

"You can't do *that*!" squeaked Norm.

"Why not?" said Grandpa. "You going to report me to the RSPCB, or something?"

"Uh?" said Norm.

"The Royal Society for the Prevention of Cruelty to Bikes?"

"Pardon?"

"It's just a *bike*, Norman. It hasn't got *feelings*."

"I know," said Norm. "But…"

"It won't feel any *pain*," said Grandpa.

Norm sighed. The *bike* might not feel any pain. But *he* flipping would. The bike was almost like his *baby*. Not that Norm actually *knew* what it was like to have a baby, of course. Although he *had* once gone four days without having a poo. Which can't have been **all** that different. But that wasn't the point, thought Norm. The point was that Grandpa was actually going to **hit** his bike! With a flipping hammer!

"You **do** want to go biking today?" said Grandpa.

Norm nodded forlornly.

"Well, I'm afraid there's no alternative," said Grandpa, heading for the door.

"Where are you going?" said Norm.

"To get a hammer."

"But..."

"What?" said Grandpa.

"There's one over there," said Norm, pointing to the workbench, where indeed there *was* a hammer, together with various other instruments of medieval torture. Or at least that's what Grandpa's tools were beginning to look like to Norm. In fact, all of a sudden the whole place seemed more like a flipping *laboratory* than a *shed* in an allotment. All Grandpa needed was a white coat and he'd look like a mad scientist about to carry out some kind of evil experiment. And in a way, thought Norm, he flipping well *was*!

60

"Oh, I'm going to need a much bigger hammer than **that**!" said Grandpa, disappearing into the sunlight. "Wait there, Norman. I'll be back in a few minutes!"

Norm thought for a moment. Frankly, he didn't fancy waiting **one** more minute, let alone a flipping **few**. Especially if the only **reason** he was waiting was so that Grandpa could start knocking lumps out of his bike with a whacking great hammer! That just wasn't going to happen, as far as Norm was concerned. There just **had** to be another way.

What was that expression? A friend in need is a friend indeed? Or was it a friend indeed is a friend in **need**? Well, whatever it was, thought Norm, taking his phone out of his pocket, he **kind** of knew what it meant. It meant that if there was one person in the whole wide world he could turn to right now, that person was the person he'd known since they were both in nappies and playing pirates and dinosaurs together at nursery. His best friend, Mikey. Mikey would know what to do. He always did. Which was a **bit** annoying, but what the heck? thought Norm. Now wasn't the time to get all bitter and twisted. There'd be plenty of time for that later.

Norm punched a couple of keys and waited. And waited. And waited. But there was no reply. So much for a flipping friend in need being a friend indeed, or whichever way round it was, thought Norm. Didn't Mikey **know** that he was trying to get hold of him? Some people were just **so** flipping inconsiderate.

It was only when Norm tried to dial again that he noticed his phone battery was flatter than a thin-crust Margherita pizza. Even **without** the extra mozzarella. Which wouldn't have happened if his parents weren't so flipping stingy and he'd had a **decent** phone in the **first** flipping place instead of some prehistoric old thing that wouldn't have looked out of place in a flipping **museum**.

Norm sighed wearily as he pocketed his phone again. Why was nothing ever straightforward? Why did **stuff** keep happening? Why did he always feel like he was stuck inside some kind of flipping Xbox game, having to overcome obstacles and challenges, before moving up to another level? It was **so** flipping unfair. But Norm knew that **one** thing was certain. He couldn't hang around in the allotments a second longer. He had to leave right now. And he had to take his beloved bike with him!

CHAPTER 6

It only **used** to take Norm a couple of minutes to get to Mikey's house, back in the days when they'd lived just round the corner from one another. But not any more. Not since Norm and his family had moved and they now lived round **lots** of

corners from one another. Or rather, not since they'd **had** to move and started eating own-brand Coco Pops because they were cheaper than **proper** Coco Pops. Now, instead of taking maybe **one** song on his iPod, it could take as many as four or five songs. And that was when

Norm was actually *riding* his bike and not wheeling it beside him as he walked. Or *trying* to wheel it beside him. Which wasn't proving easy, what with the wheel being so wonky. And not that Norm was listening to his iPod anyway. But that wasn't the point. The point was that it took even longer than usual for Norm to get to Mikey's house that morning. And if Norm had known that Mikey wasn't going to be in, he wouldn't have bothered in the first place.

Flipping typical, thought Norm, standing on Mikey's front doorstep and ringing the bell for the fifth or sixth time. Where on earth was he? It was *Saturday*. And the two of them *always* went biking on Saturdays. It was the law. Well, not really. But it may as well have been. Mikey couldn't simply have forgotten, could he? Because Norm would have forgotten his own flipping *name* before he ever forgot that he was going *biking*. Well, wherever Mikey was, thought Norm, he'd better have a pretty good excuse. Because if not? He might well be on the lookout for a new best friend by the end of the day.

Norm was so lost in thought that he didn't even hear a car pull up next to the house, let alone various car doors opening and slamming shut again.

"Hello, Norman!" said a voice.

"Uh?" said Norm, swivelling round. "Oh, hi, Mikey's dad. Hi, Mikey's mum."

"Hello, Norman," laughed Mikey's mum, who'd always found this habit of Norm's rather sweet and endearing.

"Hi, Norm," said Mikey. "I tried to call you. You must have had your phone switched off or something."

But Norm didn't reply. He wasn't even listening any more. He was scarcely aware of anything at all. He only had eyes for **one** thing.

"What's that, Mikey?"

"What's what?" said Mikey innocently, although he had a pretty good idea what Norm was referring to.

"That!" said Norm.

Mikey didn't need to turn around to know what Norm was looking at. But he did anyway.

"A car?"

"What?" said Norm irritably. "No. I meant, what's that on **top** of the car?"

"Oh, right," said Mikey. "Erm, a bike."

"I can see it's a **bike**, you doughnut," said Norm. "Is it a new bike?"

Mikey shrugged. "Dunno. Might be."

"**Might** be?" said Norm. "Or it is?"

"It is," said Mikey, beginning to look more uncomfortable by the second.

Norm hesitated. He already knew the answer even **before** he'd asked the question. "Is it for **you**, Mikey?"

Mikey nodded sheepishly.

Norm felt like he'd just run slap bang into a solid brick wall and that all the air had suddenly been knocked out of his lungs.

This was unbe-flipping-*lievable*! **Mikey** had a new **bike**? An actual new bike? Norm was the one who was mad about biking, not Mikey. Norm was the one who was constantly drooling over bikes on the internet, not Mikey. And Norm was the one who dreamt of becoming World Mountain Biking Champion, not Mikey. If anyone deserved a new bike it was **him**, not Mikey! In fact, never mind **deserved**. It was Norm who actually **needed** a new bike, not Mikey! And there was no flipping chance of **that** happening anytime soon. Not as long as his skinflint parents had anything to do with it there wasn't, anyway. And he

was stuck with **them** for a good while yet. It was so unfair. Even by Norm's standards. Because when it came to things being unfair, Norm had been there, done that and got the flipping T-shirt. But this **really** took the biscuit. In fact, never mind **biscuit**, thought Norm. **This** took the whole flipping **packet**!

"Oops," said Mikey's dad, noticing Norm's buckled front wheel. "Looks like **you** could do with a new bike, too, Norman."

You don't **say**, thought Norm. But he didn't say it.

"Whoa," said Mikey, noticing the wheel, as well. "How did you manage to do **that**?"

Gordon flipping Bennet, thought Norm. How did Mikey flipping **think** he'd done it?

"Did you crash, Norman?" asked Mikey's mum.

"Yeah," said Norm.

"Are you OK?" asked Mikey's dad.

Norm thought for a moment. Was he OK? No, he flipping **wasn't** OK, actually! As a matter of fact, he was anything **but** OK!

"I mean, did you **hurt** yourself?" said Mikey's dad, sensing that all was not well with Norm.

"I'm fine, thanks," said Norm.

"What about biking today?" said Mikey. "I was…"

Mikey stopped mid-sentence.

"What?" said Norm. "Hoping to test your **new** bike out?"

Mikey looked a bit embarrassed and gave a slight nod.

"How about you lend Norman your **old** bike, Mikey?" said Mikey's mum.

Norm and Mikey exchanged glances.

"Hey, that's a terrific idea!" said Mikey's dad. "How about it, guys?"

"Erm, yeah, why not?" said Mikey. "As long as **you're** OK with that, Norm?"

It was a good question, thought Norm. **Was** he OK with that? It was certainly a neat solution to the problem. He couldn't very well go biking on his **own** bike. Not at the moment he couldn't, anyway. And now Mikey had a **spare** one. On the one hand it was a complete no-brainer. On the other hand...

But before Norm had a chance to dwell too much about what may or may not have been on the other hand, there was a sudden beeping of a car horn. Everyone turned around to see Norm's mum and dad's car stopping at the end of the drive, and his dad staring out of the driver's side window with a face like thunder.

"Gordon flipping **Bennet**," muttered Norm, suddenly remembering what he was really supposed to be doing. Or at least what he'd been **told** to do, anyway. Judging by his dad's expression, he wasn't the **only** one who'd remembered, either.

"Hi, folks!" called Mikey's dad, with a cheery wave of his hand.

Norm's dad waved back, somewhat less cheerily. So too did Norm's mum, sitting beside him in the front of the car. Meanwhile in the rear, Brian and Dave were bouncing about, with John wedged between them, like the filling in a Cockapoo sandwich.

"I don't think your dad's too happy, Norm," said Mikey, as Norm's dad lowered his window.

"*Really*?" said Norm.

Mikey pulled a face. "Are you being sarcastic?"

"*No*," said Norm, sarcastically.

"Norman?" called Norm's dad.

"Yeah?" said Norm.

"Home. *Now*."

Norm sighed. "Coming."

"See you later then, Norm," said Mikey.

"I wouldn't count on it," grumbled Norm, trudging slowly down the drive, wheeling his bike wonkily beside him.

CHAPTER 7

By the time Norm eventually got home again and had put his wonky, useless bike back in the garage, the whole family were gathered in the front room, awaiting his arrival. **Including** John.

"We're in here," called Norm's mum the second he stepped into the hall, although Norm already had a pretty good idea where everybody was because he could **smell** them. Well, the dog and his brothers, anyway.

"Nice of you to join us," said Norm's dad, as Norm walked through the door.

"But..." began Brian.

"Sssshhhh!" whispered Dave. "I think he's being ironic."

Brian pulled a face. "What?"

Norm sighed. He wished that whatever was about to happen would hurry up and flipping happen. What was the point in dragging things out and prolonging the agony any longer? It was obvious that he was in trouble. The question was, how *much* trouble? And, more importantly, what were the consequences going to be? Because there were *bound* to be flipping consequences. There always flipping *were*.

"So?" said Norm's dad, when it became clear that Norm wasn't going to say anything without being prompted first.

"What?" said Norm.

"What do you mean **what**?" said Norm's dad, the vein on the side of his head beginning to throb. Not that Norm noticed. "You had **one** job!"

Yeah, thought Norm. And that was one more job than his **dad** had. But now probably wasn't the best time to mention that.

Norm's dad shook his head in exasperation. "What are we going to do with you, Norman?"

"Ooh, I've got an idea!" said Brian, sticking his hand up.

"Shut up, Brian, you little freak!" hissed Norm.

"Language," said Dave.

WOOF! went John.

"Quiet!" said Norm's mum. "All of you!"

Norm's dad exhaled slowly and noisily. "Where *were* you?"

Norm shrugged. "Out."

"I know you were *out*, Norman!"

Norm pulled a face. So if he *knew*, why flipping ask then?

"What were you *thinking*, love?" said Norm's mum. "You *know* you were supposed to stay in."

"Yeah, I know," said Norm. "But..."

"But you *didn't*," said Norm's dad, interjecting. "You deliberately disobeyed us."

"Yeah, I know, but..." Norm stopped.

"But *what*?" said Norm's dad.

Norm thought for a moment. "It's Chelsea's fault."

"What?" said Norm's dad, incredulously.

"It's not *my* fault," said Norm. "She said she'd look out for the parcel."

Norm's dad laughed. "I don't believe this."

"It's true," said Norm. "*She* did."

"And that was very nice of her," said Norm's mum, intervening before Norm could dig

80

himself any deeper and before Norm's
dad blew a fuse.

Norm's dad shook his head again.

"Would you like to know what was **in** the
parcel?" said Norm's mum.

"What?" said
Norm. "You mean
it arrived?"

"Here," said Norm's
mum, producing a
small packet from
behind her back
and holding it out to
Norm.

"But..."

"Take it."

Norm took it.

"Open it," said his mum.

Norm opened it.

"It's a phone," said Norm's mum.

Norm could see that it was a phone. "Yeah, but..."

"It's for **you**, love."

Norm looked at his mum as if she'd suddenly sprouted an extra head. "What?"

"It's for **you**. I saw it on one of the shopping channels. It's not exactly the latest model. But it was a bargain."

"But…" began Norm.

"What?" said Norm's mum. "Don't you want it?"

"No! No!" said Norm quickly. "I mean, yes, yes! I really, **really** want it! I just don't know what to say."

"How about 'thank you'?" said Norm's dad.

"What?" said Norm. "I mean, yeah. I mean **thanks**, Mum!"

Norm's mum smiled. "That's OK, love."

Norm looked at the phone. His mum was right. It **wasn't** exactly the latest model. Far from it, in fact. But, right now, Norm

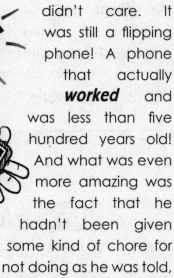

didn't care. It was still a flipping phone! A phone that actually **worked** and was less than five hundred years old! And what was even more amazing was the fact that he hadn't been given some kind of chore for not doing as he was told, or that he hadn't been grounded for the rest of his life. Maybe today wasn't going to be **quite** so bad after all!

"Cooee!" said a voice from the hall. "Anyone in?"

"YEAH! GRANDPA!" yelled Brian and Dave in unison.

"Front room, Dad!" called Norm's mum.

"Ah, *there* you are, Norman," said Grandpa, appearing in the doorway a moment later and holding a huge hammer. "I wondered where you'd got to. Let's get that bike of yours fixed, shall we?"

Gordon flipping **Bennet**, thought Norm.

THE END

WANT MORE NORM?

DON'T MISS ANY OF THE HILARIOUS ACTION IN THESE GREAT BOOKS!

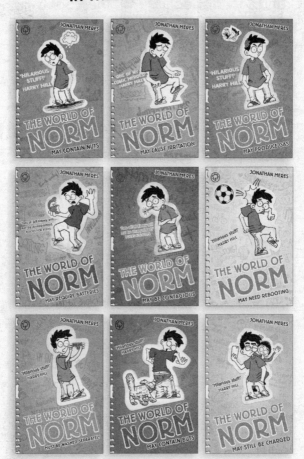

AND - **COMING IN MAY** -
THE WORLD OF NORM: INCLUDES DELIVERY

THE WORLD OF
NORM

MAY CONTAIN PRIZES

HELLO, NORM FANS. DO YOU WANT TO WIN A BRAND-NEW BIKE? YES, THAT'S RIGHT. A BRAND-NEW, SHINY BIKE!

Norm World Book Day competition!

- Go to the World of Norm website at: www.worldofnorm.co.uk

- Enter the competition

- You may win a prize!

Closing date: 30/04/2016
See website for full terms and conditions.

Max Helsing knew it was
going to be one of those days
when... He was attacked by a
GHOUL.

by Curtis Jobling

Read on for a taste of this
MONSTROUSLY brilliant new series
from Orchard Books...

'It's not like I go looking for trouble,' said Max as he approached the top corner of Gallows Hill Burying Ground, with his best friend Syd riding beside him. 'But I always seem to land in it.' He pulled on his brakes and sat up in his saddle, craning his neck as he looked through the railings. The cemetery was cloaked in mist, headstones rising like jagged mountain peaks through a blanket of clouds.

'What is it?' asked Syd.

'Not sure,' muttered Max. 'Something.'

'Could be nothing.'

'Nope.'

'How do you know it isn't?'

'Call it a hunch,' replied Max. He hopped off his bike and continued on foot.

Syd begrudgingly parked her bike alongside Max's. 'I know all about your hunches.'

His instincts, which Max had once jokingly referred to as his 'Helsey sense tingling', were guiding him toward the source of his hunch. He occasionally got a gut feeling when something monstrous or magical was approaching. He never knew what the danger might be – only that it was impending. He picked a path between the graves, occasionally stopping to get his bearings. Max took a turn and headed deeper into the burying ground, smoky tendrils of mist swirling about them. He was slowing now and gradually came to a halt.

It sounded like a big dog feeding in the darkness, a low growl hidden behind a grinding noise. Max reached into his bag, fished a plastic rod out and snapped it. The high-intensity glow stick shone white, illuminating the area with a crackling light.

The grave was old, the headstone weather-beaten and its occupant's identity illegible. Turf was piled high around it, splinters of ancient timber half buried in the earth. Max took another step forward to throw more light into the crudely excavated pit. He nodded.

'Well, that figures.'

A naked creature straddled the broken coffin. It was an emaciated humanoid, hideously desiccated, leathery skin drawn tight over wasted muscles and joints. The odd wisp of white hair still clung to its blotchy scalp, but it had long ago departed the world of the living. In its skeletal hands it held two halves of a human femur, gnawing on it, the brittle bone already snapped in two like a stick of celery. As the light fell on it, the monster ceased its feeding to look up. Unmistakeably undead, its pale eyes shone back eerily, reflecting the glow stick, black pinprick pupils focused on Max. It ground its teeth together in its lipless mouth.

'Out you come,' said Max, clicking his fingers and pointing to the turf beside the grave. 'And you can tidy this mess up while you're at it.'

Syd peered over Max's shoulder, using the monster hunter as a human shield. 'Zombie?'

'Nope. Ghoul, and a young one, too, I reckon. Still got a bit of hair left, and it's not completely blind yet. Probably rose . . . let's see, fifty years ago?'

The creature clapped its crooked teeth together, gums exposed. Max grinned.

'You appear to be hiding behind me,' he said over his shoulder, chuckling. 'Ghouls are carrion feeders. They're relatively harmless.'

'Relatively is the key word there. Who knows

GHOUL, LESSER

ORIGIN: Persia

STRENGTHS: Feels no pain, immune to most physical attacks.

WEAKNESS: Head shots and daylight.

HABITAT: Burial grounds, often nesting in large groups in subterranean tunnel systems.

These relatively harmless monsters are associated with graveyards and the consumption of corpses, their principal diet. Although undead, they provide little danger to the living, only feeding upon decayed flesh. Not to be confused with the infinitely more dangerous <u>zombie</u>.

—Erik Van Helsing, March 16th, 1851

PHYSICAL FIELD ACCOUNT-
THE GETTYSBURG GHOULS
The unmistakeable stench of the foul fiends reveals their location long before one encounters them. Their tunnel system is ingenious, carrying them beneath each grave so they may feed upon the war dead without fear of discovery by the living. Unable to reason with them, I have reluctantly resorted to the blade. I have laboured for two weeks dispatching them, the President and his company oblivious to my presence, and rightly so.

— Esme Van Helsing, November 24th, 1863

GRANDPA had a serious problem with ghouls. He got it WAY WRONG - they are HARMLESS!!

MAX HELSING

Feb 27th, 2015

The only good ghoul is a dead ghoul. Do not be lulled into a false sense of security by this devil. It is a wicked, soulless demon, no doubt in league with the rest of its undead brethren.

— Algernon Van Helsing, July 15th, 1936

where that thing's been?' Syd wrinkled her nose and shoved Max forward. 'Do your thing and let's get out of here. Chop, chop.'

Max turned back to the ghoul in the grave. The creature raised a hand through the air and raked at him, rising unsteadily on its filthy, clawed feet. Max leaned back.

'Hey, cut that out. Now, we can do this the easy way or the hard way. I've had a pretty lousy day, so I'd rather we go with the former. I need you to put the bones back exactly as you found them – well, the parts you haven't already eaten, anyway – and then haul your skinny butt outta there. Then you've got to fill this earth back in. I know, I know, chores are a drag, so how 'bout Syd and I help you, OK? Teamwork always gets a job done!'

Whether the ghoul understood Max was entirely unclear, but the boy continued regardless, giving the monster every opportunity to do the right thing.

'So, whaddaya say? You going to do what I ask?'

The ghoul snarled and turned its back on

him, reaching back into the coffin to rip loose a clutch of ribs. Max sighed in resignation.

'Why do they never choose the easy way?' he asked, reaching back into the messenger bag and fishing around for what he needed. Grabbing the crucifix, Max presented it with a flourish and began the ritual, words of Latin spilling forth. The ghoul was instantly scrambling, gurgling as it went, seizing the headstone to drag itself up. Syd let loose an involuntary squeal, backing away as the monster squirmed out of the pit.

The ghoul landed in the pile of soil, writhing and kicking as Max continued chanting, the crucifix glinting in the dim light where it rose from his knuckles. Crawling now, the beast drew closer to the shadows and the mist.

'That's right, run along and tell your pals I'd better not see them here, either. Gallows Hill Burying Ground is off-limits, Bones. I see you here again, I may not play so nice!'

'Well done,' said Syd. 'For a moment there, you almost sounded like a real Van Helsing.'

'And you almost sounded like a real girl. Where did that squeal come from?'

'I'll never get used to the monsters,' said Syd. 'I'm the Q to your 007 – fieldwork ain't my thing. Now can we go?'

'This grave still needs filling,' said Max, tossing his jacket onto the headstone. He started shoving the dirt back into the ground with his hands. 'You could help and we'd be done quicker. Many hands make light work.'

With a grumble, Syd joined her friend, kneeling in the soil and setting to the task.

'You know, back in the bad old days, your dad would've just lopped its head off.'

'Well,' said Max, throwing an armful of mud onto the splintered coffin, 'I'm not my dad.'

'That's something all monsters should be grateful for.'

Want more? Don t miss
MAX HELSING: MONSTER HUNTER.
Out May 2016

WORLD BOOK DAY fest

WORLD
BOOK
DAY
3 MARCH 2016

Want to **READ** more?

 VISIT

YOUR LOCAL BOOKSHOP

- Get some great recommendations for what to read next
- Meet your favourite authors & illustrators at brilliant events
- Discover books you never even knew existed!

 FIND YOUR LOCAL BOOKSHOP
www.booksellers.org.uk/bookshopsearch

 JOIN

YOUR LOCAL LIBRARY

You can browse and borrow from a HUGE selection of books and get recommendations of what to read next from expert librarians—all for **FREE**! You can also discover libraries' wonderful children's and family reading activities.

 FIND YOUR LOCAL LIBRARY
www.findalibrary.co.uk

 GET ONLINE

VISIT **WORLDBOOKDAY.COM** TO DISCOVER A WHOLE NEW WORLD OF BOOKS!

- Downloads and activities for top books and authors
- Cool games, trailers and videos
- Author events in your area
- News, competitions and new books—all in a FREE monthly email

AND MORE!